Custom Car

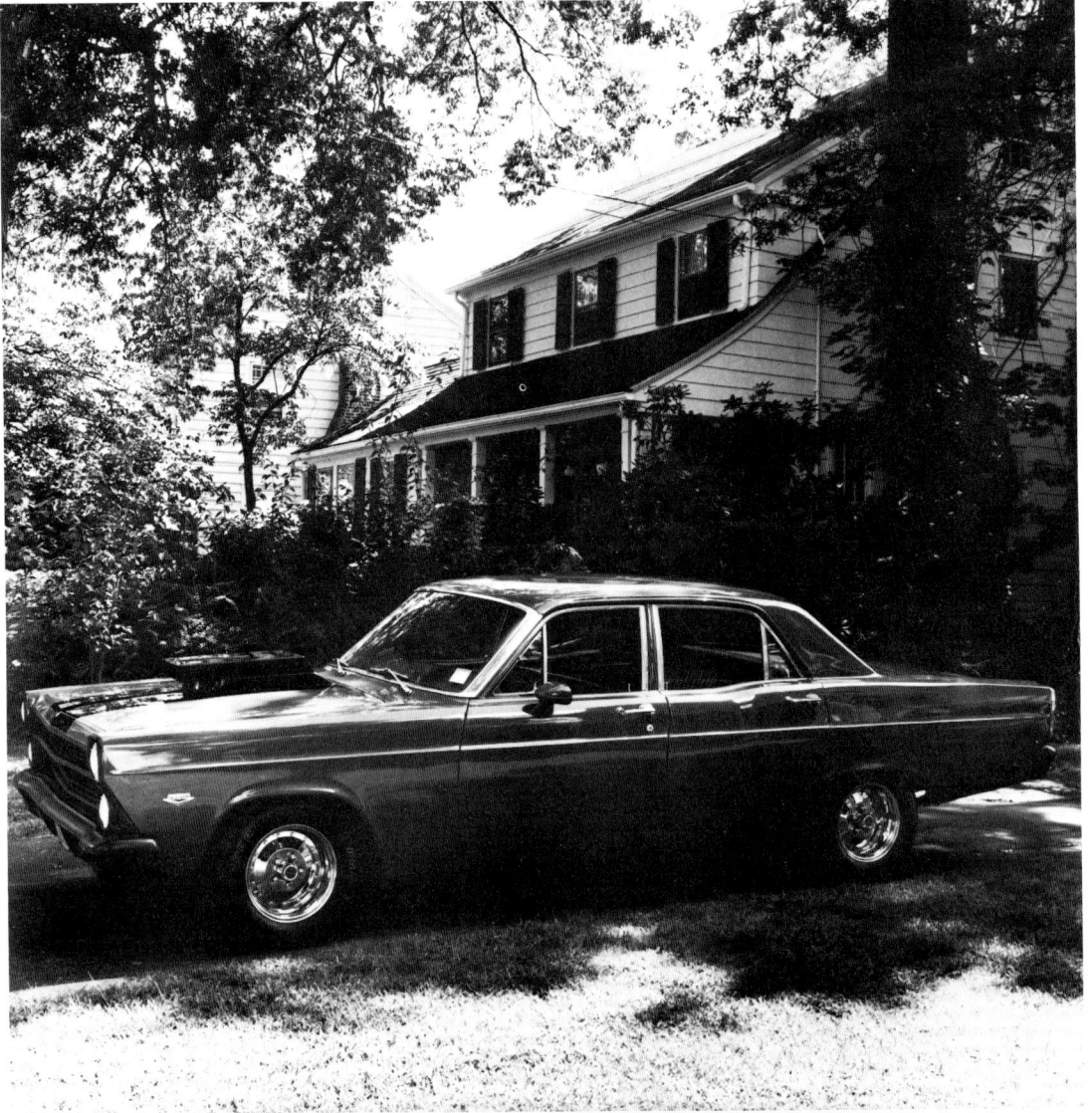

Custom Car

A NUTS-AND-BOLTS GUIDE TO CREATING ONE

Jim Murphy

Technical Consultant: TOM WALSH

CLARION BOOKS / NEW YORK

The following brand names mentioned in the text are registered trademarks: Nova, Ford, Snap-on Tools, MAC Tools, Holley, Hooker, Cooper, Cragar.

Clarion Books
a Houghton Mifflin Company imprint
52 Vanderbilt Avenue, New York, NY 10017

Library of Congress Cataloging-in-Publication Data
Murphy, Jim, 1947–
Custom car: a nuts-and-bolts guide to creating one.
Includes index.
Summary: Describes how an ordinary family car may
be transformed, on a limited budget, into a unique
custom car.
1. Automobiles—Customizing—Juvenile literature.
[1. Automobiles—Customizing] I. Title.
TL255.M87 1989   629.28′722   86-33352
ISBN 0-89919-272-6

P 10 9 8 7 6 5 4 3 2 1

To Carol—Thanks for your patient understanding and encouragement.

J.M.

For Tommy—Never lose sight of your dreams.

T.W.

Contents

Introduction

You hear the rumble first. It's an engine, low, throaty, unmistakably powerful. When you turn to check it out, your eyes rivet on a dazzling yellow machine with hood scoop, blacked-out windows, and gleaming chrome wheels. What is it? A custom car!

Technically, any car that has had its engine, interior, and exterior modified could be considered a custom car. The trouble with this definition is that it's too tame. Custom cars accent power — in color, styling, and engine horsepower. And since the owner alters the car to match his or her tastes and personality, the result is a truly unique, one-of-a-kind machine.

Custom Car shows how a very ordinary family car was totally transformed. You'll see the work involved as well as the many decisions and compromises that had to be made along the way. As a challenge, we set a spending limit of $5,500. This is a hefty chunk of cash, no doubt about it. But if you consider that we were going to rebuild the entire engine, repair and paint the exterior, and redo the interior — in short, create a completely new car — it isn't very much at all. At the back of the book you'll find a Glossary of car terms in case you come across any unfamiliar ones, as well as a complete Price List for parts and tools.

All that's left now is to get this show into gear.

Finding the Right Car

1

The most logical place to start any custom car project is with the car itself. Why logical? Because decisions about what to do with the car and the parts needed to do it depend on the car's make, model, and year.

Ordinarily, customizers prefer to work on two-door hardtops, called *coupes*. Novas, Chevy IIs, Chevelles, and Challengers are some of the most popular models. Coupes are small and light, which means any horsepower added to the engine isn't wasted on moving unnecessary weight. Coupes are generally designed more aerodynamically, allowing them to knife through the air more easily than a four-door car. And when the rear end is jacked up and wide tires put on, these chunky cars take on a fierce, determined look. More importantly, the popularity of these cars makes getting parts relatively easy.

But the popularity of these cars is also their biggest drawback. The demand for them keeps their resale value high. It's not unusual to find a fifteen-year-old Nova in good condition costing over $1,000. That kind of price tag can put a big dent in any customizer's budget.

Finding a car to work on shouldn't be too difficult. Check the "For Sale" section of your local and area newspapers, or pick up a magazine devoted to car sales. You're bound to find several likely candidates. Then go look at the cars, comparing price and condition.

Before pulling out your wallet, here are a few things to remember. You'll probably be buying an older car, one that's ten or more years old with lots of miles on the odometer. The potential problems a car might have multiply with age and wear—rust eats away at the body, the steering mechanism loosens, the clutch wears out. The list is endless. You'll want to be sure to check every inch of the car, top and bottom, inside and out. If at all possible, bring along someone who really knows about cars and who will look over the car carefully.

After a thorough curbside check, be sure you (and your expert) road test the car. You'll be able to hear how the engine works, listen for problems in the transmission and clutch, feel the way the car rides and takes turns. Be very wary if the owner doesn't want you to take the car out on a road test.

The best way to avoid buying a car loaded with potential problems is to arm yourself with information. Go to the library and check out several books on how to buy a used car. Much of the information in these books is really just common sense, such as never to inspect a car at night. But some of the tips can be helpful. One book gives a series of questions to ask over the phone to avoid having to inspect every car in person. Another lists fifteen key things to look for when examining a car, such as various kinds of fluid leaks and what they could mean. You might be very eager to get started on your car work, but a modest amount of patience and research can spare you a lot of costly, annoying surprises.

In our case, another person's misfortune turned out to be a stroke of luck for us. One day, the mother of a friend was calmly tooling down a road in her 1967 Ford Fairlane when a dried-out gas hose sprung a leak. The gas dripped onto the engine and ignited, and in seconds the entire engine compartment was engulfed in flames. The woman escaped unharmed, but by the time fire fighters put it out, the fire had destroyed almost everything under the hood.

Cars that have had engine fires are usually towed to a wrecker and crushed for scrap metal. Fortunately, we learned about the Fairlane before this happened and were able to check out the car.

Despite an abundance of ugly chrome and a good deal of body rust and damage, the car's basic lines were clean and sharp. The Fairlane is also light for a four door. In fact, Fairlanes were designed by Ford in the early 1960s to replace the gigantic and extremely heavy Ford Galaxie models used on the stock car racing circuit. While the engine in our car was a charred mess, the engine block — the single most expensive part of the engine — was uncracked and usable.

We had another reason for wanting to work on the Fairlane. Custom car magazines and customizers seem to have a passionate aversion to four-door cars. Most early model four doors are ungainly monsters, though the Fairlane is pretty light. Four-door cars are also viewed as "family" cars — a conservative image that suggests the cars are slow. We wanted to prove that our four-door "family" car could be transformed into an eye-catching, sleek street machine.

If all of this weren't enough, there was something else we liked about the Fairlane. The price was right: $75. We felt that the money saved on the purchase price of the car could be used to make it look and run better. So we paid the woman and had our car towed home.

CHEVELLE

'81 CHEVY MALIBU
4 dr., auto, ac, ps, 6 cyl., radials, 69,000 miles, $2795.

Call 337-5110
OAKLAND MOTOR CAR

71 4 DR. CHEVELLE , new tires, new batt., new exh., 64k orig. miles, good cond., asking $600., Call 201-773-4812 from 10am to 7pm. Garfield

1968 CHEVELLE SS 327 eng., 4 spd. hurst shifter, 12 bolt posi rear, holly carb., blk and gold, blk int., chrome whls., new vinyl roof, new clutch and brks., 6 guages, fiberglass hood, 6' scoop, $4200, Call 201-750-1464 before 3 pm. Woodbridge

1969 BIG BLOCK CHEVELLE brand new motor, new trans., 411 rear, $2500 or bo. 201-933-4866 after 2 pm. Woodridge

1968 CHEVELLE Super Sport, 427 C.I.D., black on black, 4 spd., 4..10 rear, more details for muscle car enthusiats, $6600 Firm. Call days 2 0 1 - 4 8 8 - 8 1 4 9 o r e v e s. 201-944-6161. River Edge

65 CHEVELLE MALIBU , v8, 283ci, 112,000 miles, engine still running strong, NEW: battery, ign switch, fuel pump, timing chain, rear springs, lower ball joints, idler arm, body needs work, oil leaks slowly, call 609-443-8118 (or 609-452-3208 ask for Sarah) $250. Cranbury,

72 MALIBU with 77 engine, 350, eng. rebuilt, new tires, must see, asking $3000. or bo, call 201-827-0802 Franklin

1980 CHEVY 4 DR. Malibu], ac, auto., nice car, $1800., Call 201-543-6121 eves. Mendham

75 CHEVY MALIBU , blue, 2 dr, 350 engine, 8 cyl, ac, am-fm radio, body in good cond, runs good, mileage, 95,000 plus, asking $900. or bo, call 6pm-9pm 201-863-1123 Secaucus, **80 MALIBU CLASSIC** , 6 cyl., auto., ps, pb, ac, rr defrost, amfm stereo, 56k miles, ex. cond.. new paint, new

1975 CHEVY MALIBU , ps, pb, 41,000 orig. mi., recently passed inspection. $500 or BO. 201-838-9156 Butler

1979 MALIBU brown, 3 spd., 6 cyl., ac, amfm 123K, one owner, new shocks, brakes and tires, asking $995. Call Days 201-631-7539 or Eves 201-377-7505 Florham Park

72 CHEVELLE 6 cyl. runs great, very reliable, needs new brakes. $250 or bo 201-789-0926 after 5pm Garwood

71 CHEVELLE, NEEDS TRANS, $350. 201-376-9020 Springfield

71 CHEVY MALIBU V8, ps, pb, At, am fm, D/ac front disc brakes, rebuilt trans, new starter and exhaust system, carb., timing chain and lower ball joints. Runs sound. $650 201-777-3539 Wallington

79 MALIBU CLASSIC 4dr. auto, ps, pb, air, rear defrost, small V8, gd on gas, many new parts, asking $1300. or bo, must sell, call aft. 6pm 201-344-5970 Newark

1972 CHEVELLE 307 motor. Air. Runs good. Body in pretty good shape. $600 Call Eves 201-779-5395 or 201-288-6091 days. Hasbrouck Heights

1972 CHEVELLE , white w/SS stripes,350 engine, auto, ac,Holley carb,hooker headers,new dual exhaust, new brakes, runs exc.,$950 or bo. Call 201-684-4786 after 6PM. Mahwah

1973 CHEVROLET MALIBU , 4 dr, 8 cyl, good transportation, $295., call 201-447-2705 leave message. Wyckoff,

64 CHEVELLE MALIBU SS 2 dr.hardtop, 6 cyl. auto on floor, with console. Bucket seats. Red with white top, black int., excell. cond. throughout. $1500 or ob 201-691-2762 Hackettstown

1974 CHEVELLE 350, 4 BBL, some chrome, auto., bucket seats, new paint, clean int., red int. and ext., alum. slots, bo around $2500. 201-382-2134 Rahway

70 CHEVY CHEVELLE SS 396 Holly 750 double pumper 4 spd, posi rear, brand new M21 trans, new Mc-Cloud 3 finger pressure plate and

1982 CHEVROLET MALIBU Classic Sport Sedan. 4 dr., V6, auto., ac, ps, pb, amfm, plus Rusty Jones & more. Light blue metallic, 26,000 mi. orig. owner, retired Executive, second car, superb cond. throughout $4795. 201-766-6446 Basking Ridge

1969 CHEVY CHEVELLE, 350 engine, rebuilt, recorder cam, asking $1200. Call 201-584-4181. Succasunna

1974 MALIBU CLASSIC , 2 dr, 350 engine, 350 trans, ac, 59,000 orig miles, one owner, good cond, first $500 takes it. Call 201-635-9849 btwn 8am-5pm Mon-Sun. Chatham Twnsp

72 CHEVELLE 250, V6, $400 or b/o, call 201-964-3713 after 6pm Union

CHEVY II-NOVA

1974 CHEVY NOVA , very dependable and economical,exc. int,minor dents,just passed inspection, $800 or bo. CAll 201-267-3669 ask for Jeff. New Vernon

67 NOVA SUPER SPORT Chevy II. Exc. Restoration project. Need quarter panels. First $850 takes it 201-492-8366 West Mllford

75 NOVA CUSTOM , 350 trans. and eng., 4 bbl., alum. intake, runs great, also have rear Cragar SST 60 tires, plus snows, and some chrome on eng., its quick, $2100. or best offer, Call 201-772-7789 after 3pm. Clifton

1972 CHEVROLET NOVA 2 door, 6 cyl, good condt., burns no oil, has new tires, new battery, plus other new parts. Asking $650 or BO. 201-322-6896 aft. 6pm Fanwood

75 CHEVY NOVA , grey with red interior, $1500. Call 201-354-6913 or 926-8461, days. Hillside

77 CHEVY NOVA , V8 305, 2 dr., clean in and out, am/fm 8-track, ps, pb, ac, low miles, ask $1000, call 201-857-5079 after 6pm (mon.-fri.) Ferona

'75 CHEVY NOVA , 6 cyl. for parts Only or whole car. $300. 201-850-3405 or 201-852-9313 Hackettstown

---

Here is a typical "For Sale" section from a magazine completely devoted to selling cars. A careful study will reveal a wide price range, from a $200 fixer-upper to a fully equipped muscle-car at $6,600.

When we opened the hood of the Fairlane, this is what we found. Wires and hoses were charred and blistered, the distributor cap had melted—in short, this looked more like a barbecue grill than an engine.

The intense fire had burned the paint on the hood and had left an ugly scar. Even so, the square look of the front seemed clean and aggressive.

A side view shows where soot from the hood dripped down the left front fender. In addition, the heavy aluminum moldings, areas of rust, and many scratches and dents make the Fairlane a sorry sight. This is the time to use your imagination, to "see" what the car might be like repaired and painted — and to estimate what the expenses might be.

2

Getting Your (Car) Act Together

The Fairlane was sitting in the driveway, its engine useless and a tire leaking air. It looked pathetic. Everything in us wanted to get the car quickly running again. However, we checked the impulse to plunge right in. The wisest approach would be to figure out precisely what we wanted to do to the car. With goals firmly in mind, we could establish a work schedule and purchase parts and tools when we needed them. To figure out our game plan, we needed lots of information.

Car magazines are the handiest sources of current information about customizing. *Car Craft* and *Custom Car* are two of the more popular magazines, although others may be available in your area. Most supermarkets and drugstores will have the latest issues, and many libraries have subscriptions to car magazines.

These magazines provide two valuable kinds of information. First, each issue contains a number of stories focusing on specific car projects. A recent issue of *Car Craft* looked at eight different cars, detailing how the engine, transmission, steering, suspension, interior, and exterior of each was changed and documenting the alterations with photos. You'll also find many technical articles covering such things as carburetors, manifolds, body work—in short, every aspect of car modification.

Advertisements are the other source of information contained in these magazines. Most ads we come across in our lives are a nuisance, flashy come-ons designed to make you remember the product's name but giving little useful information. Custom car magazines have their share of these, but they also contain ads for technical books on car modification as well as ads for parts and tools. And almost all of these ads give specific prices. It's possible to assemble an entire engine on paper and see precisely what it might cost you.

Studying magazine articles and ads will give you a good foundation of knowledge, but it's only the first step. Eventually, you'll want to visit a few speed shops. There you'll actually get to see a wide variety of parts, from aluminum manifolds to chrome wheels to tail pipes and steering wheels. Compare the prices you find at these stores with those in the magazines to find the best values.

Don't be afraid to ask a few questions, either. Most store owners will be happy to talk about the ins and outs of customizing, or at least refer you to someone who might help you. Remember, they're in the business of selling you parts, so they'll go out of their way to be helpful. One caution: don't get talked into buying anything until you've done a lot of research.

You might want to take in some custom car shows or drag strip swap meets. You'll get to see dazzling cars, and you'll be able to gather lots of solid information about car rebuilding, too. The manufacturer of your car is another source of information. We wrote Ford Motor Company and were told about a special magazine it put out in 1969 called *Muscle Parts*. It was out of print, and the company couldn't locate a copy of the magazine in its files, so we began our own search. After two weeks we came across someone who happened to have a copy of it. The minute we saw the magazine, we knew it was just what we needed. (More about this magazine in the next chapter.)

Bear in mind that the car you see in a book or magazine has often gone through many years of work. The engine may have gone through two or more complete modifications, the result of the owner's increasing mechanical ability and improving finances. The exterior and interior may have been designed and executed by a professional at a steep price. Feel free to dream up your ultimate car, but keep in mind your degree of skill and the size of your wallet.

You should also ask the police about local and state regulations regarding noise codes, hood scoop clearance limitations — anything that might affect your plans for modification. For instance, it is illegal to put certain types of headers on a car in California. What's the sense of building a spectacular-looking car that's illegal to drive on the street?

It's also a good idea to make some inquiries about insurance before you start to work. Most insurance companies charge higher rates for cars with high-performance engines. And trying to get fire, theft, and collision insurance can be mind-boggling. *You will absolutely need insurance,* so all you can do is call as many insurance companies as possible to see which one provides the most protection for the lowest cost.

You've spent a lot of time thinking about what you want to do with your car. You know how strong you want to make the engine; you can visualize the exterior and interior clearly. The next step is to get the parts you'll need to make this all come true. You could head for the nearest speed shop and buy them, but before you do, consider some options.

1. Scour the "For Sale" sections of your area newspapers for new or used parts. We picked up brand-new headers this way and saved about $30. Just be absolutely certain you have the

right part before you pay for it. There are no guarantees or refunds when you shop this way.

2. Ask customizers and mechanics if they know people who drive (or drove) your make of car. Other owners often have spare parts they'd be happy to sell squirreled away in their garage or basement. We found a fellow who'd had a race car with a 289 in it. In his basement, still in the original box, was a racing cam in perfect condition. He had no use for it, so he let us have it for $15, $90 off the store price.

3. Custom car shows are a great place to meet people who drive your make of car or know where parts can be had. Again, be sure you are buying the right part before you part with your money.

4. Don't forget to contact the manufacturer of your car. Ford and General Motors produce regular and high-performance parts for many of their engines, and at reasonable prices. Visit the service area of a manufacturer's dealer and ask what is available and if the dealer has a price list.

5. Junkyards can be dirty, muddy places, but they can also be treasure troves of parts. We found several items at a junkyard, including both front fenders.

6. There are always those ads in car magazines, too. Before making a purchase, call the chamber of commerce where the company is located to be sure it is reputable. And remember that there are sometimes postage and handling charges, as well as sales taxes, that can drive up what at first looks like a bargain price. Read the fine print carefully.

7. Finally, there is the J. C. Whitney auto parts and tool catalog. J. C. Whitney is the central distributor of parts and tools made by a wide variety of manufacturers. Our experience has been that the quality of what they offer is very good; what's more, they guarantee satisfaction with everything shipped. For instance, J. C. Whitney was the source of our headliner, carpet,

and seat covers. Each one of these items was as good as, or better than, what was in the Fairlane when it came off the assembly line.

You'll want to send away for a catalog as soon as possible. The catalog isn't very handsome. It's crammed with ads for parts, the type is tiny, and the illustrations are badly reproduced line drawings. But once you get used to searching through the ads, the J. C. Whitney catalog will prove a handy source. You can contact the company by writing to: J. C. Whitney & Co., 1917-19 Archer Avenue, P.O. Box 8410, Chicago, Illinois 60680.

Will you need anything else before starting? Sure. You won't be able to do anything without tools. The following is a complete list of the tools we used on the Fairlane. For convenience, we've divided the list into sections showing the tools needed to work on specific areas of the car. Those in the general category have a wide variety of uses. An asterisk appears next to tools that are expensive or are needed for a limited number of jobs — try to rent or borrow these tools.

For work on the engine
Hose clamp pliers
Cylinder hone*
Ridge reamer*
Torque wrench*
Piston ring compressor*
Piston ring groove cleaner*
Piston ring expander or
    installer*
Feeler gauge
Timing light*
Distributor wrench*

Flare nut wrenches
Gasket scraper
Oil filter wrench
Universal puller set*
Engine hoist*
Engine stand*
Floor jack*

For electrical work
Wire cutters
Test light

For brake work
Brake pliers*
Brake-adjusting spoon*

For work on the suspension
Offset pliers
Tie-rod fork*
Ball joint fork*

For upholstery work
Carpet shears
Pop (or hog) riveter
Hog-ring pliers*

For general use
Standard flathead
  screwdriver set
Phillips-head screwdriver
  set
Socket wrench sets with ⅜-,
  ½-, and ¼-inch drive with
  handles and extensions

Open-end wrench set
Combination or box wrench
  set
Electric drill and bits
Hammers
Standard pliers
Needle-nose pliers
Crowbar or pry bar
Knife or razor blades
Hacksaw
Wire brush
Allen wrenches
Adjustable pliers
Vice grip pliers
Chisels
Droplight or flashlights
Tape measure/ruler
Breaker bar
Car ramps or safety stands*

This list might seem overwhelming, but it really isn't. Most of these tools are very ordinary and can probably be found in your own basement. The more specialized ones (those marked with asterisks) can often be rented. An engine hoist can sell for $1,000 to $4,000 or more; it might rent for $35 a day, a considerable savings. Stop by several local rental stores and pick up their rental lists.

For tools you can't rent, you might try to borrow them — from neighbors, local mechanics, or friends. People are amazingly generous with tools if they aren't using them at the time and know you're serious about your work. *Just remember to return the tool the minute you're done with it and in the same condition you got it*; otherwise you'll lose a valuable source of tools forever. And don't make a pest of yourself; even the nicest individual might grow weary of always lending out things. If you find yourself borrowing frequently from someone, you might consider striking some sort of "rental agreement" with the person. We borrowed an engine stand for over three weeks; in return, we paid $20 and promised to clean the stand of years of caked-on grease and dirt.

Most likely you'll have to buy one or more tools sooner or later. Again, the "For Sale" section of newspapers might offer some great bargains, although speed shops, hardware stores, and catalogues (such as those printed by Snap-on Tools or MAC Tools) will probably have a wider choice. Our one suggestion here is to avoid very cheap brands. Such tools break easily and always at the worst time. Invest in the best and it'll pay for itself with years of use.

A final thought about buying tools. In order to spend money wisely, buy tools only when they are needed.

You've spent a lot of time researching and thinking about what kind of car you want to build. Deciding on the parts and tools you'll need, you've drawn up a plan of action that fits your budget and time schedule. What do you do now? Get out that rachet wrench and put it to work.

A recent visit to a local newsstand turned up these four magazines specifically devoted to car customizing.

Muscle Parts (center) gave us precise details on how to beef up the Fairlane's engine. While working on the car, we came across two newer magazines aimed at Ford engines. Both were loaded with specific information, part numbers, and prices.

This is a typical ad for parts from a customizing magazine. It's possible to save a good deal of money by shopping through the mail, but always read the fine print for additional costs, such as sales tax or shipping and handling charges.

We searched all around for a specific type of piston at the lowest possible price — the J. C. Whitney catalogue, the *Want Ad Press,* and car magazine ads. A speed shop turned out to offer the best deal. You have to admit the new pistons (on the left) are a startling contrast to the old and very abused ones (on the right).

We got lucky with this Holley four-barrel carburetor (on the right). We found a customizer who'd used it for less than a month before deciding to get an even bigger carburetor for his car. It was perfect for our car and was practically new, so we bought it—for half the cost of one bought at a car shop.

On the left are the catalogues for MAC Tools and Snap-on Tools. Check your local telephone directory to see where their nearest distributors are located, then try to get your hands on a catalogue and price list. On the right is an issue of the J. C. Whitney Parts and Accessories catalogue. It's a handy source of information, so get your name on their mailing list.

3

Putting the Zip Back In

It happens all too often. You spot an eye-catching street machine cruising your way. The paint job is dazzling, bright and polished to a lustrous gleam; the rear end has been jacked up, giving the car that "don't mess with me" look. It's a mean-looking machine, and you want to know what else the owner's done to his car. Then it passes by, and your enthusiasm is dampened. The engine sounds like a washing machine in desperate need of repair.

Some customizers, especially first-timers, rush to get their car painted, put on new wheels and tires, or install the best stereo they can find. Outwardly, their car looks great, but where it counts—under the hood—it's nothing but a tired, old heap. They'd like to do more work on the car, of course, but they're out of money or energy. That's why we advise revamping and beefing up the engine first.

As mentioned in the last chapter, our search for information about our Fairlane netted us the magazine *Muscle Parts* put out by Autolite-Ford Parts Division. This is a clear, no-nonsense discussion of "everything you need to know about increasing Ford engine horsepower." While this magazine is obviously for Ford engines, the general principles it covers can be applied to any make of engine.

Muscle Parts breaks engine performance levels into stages, each adding more horsepower. And since more horsepower usually means more money, you can pick your stage according to your finances. For instance, stage one calls for bolting on a high-performance carburetor, manifold, manifold gasket, and air filter. These are relatively easy changes to make and cost under $220. That isn't much at all for the additional thirty-one horsepower you'll get. Then when you have more cash, you can invest in the next stage, and so on.

We knew when we bought the Fairlane that we'd be replacing everything in the engine except the block. We decided to wring as much power as we could from the engine and still have it street legal. As noted earlier, we didn't go directly to a speed shop or a dealer to purchase parts. Instead, we searched newspapers, tramped through junkyards, and questioned every customizer we came across. In the space of two months, we rounded up a wiring harness, a Holley four-barrel carburetor, a racing cam, a set of Hooker headers, and rebuilt heads with solid lifters. We estimate we saved $385 over store prices. When we had exhausted every avenue, we went to the speed shops and dealers, always careful to get the best price possible. Now we were ready to put the wrench to work.

Taking apart an engine is one of the easiest jobs imaginable. Rachet wrench, pliers, screwdrivers, hammers, and a lot of elbow grease can get everything loosened in an afternoon.

Here are some guidelines to follow.

1. *Take your time.* If you try to loosen bolts and screws too quickly, especially ones that might be rusted tight, you run the risk of slipping and gouging your knuckles. And you don't want to strip bolt heads, break off bolts, or damage usable parts.

2. *Be organized.* When you remove the engine bolts, for example, put them in a container and label it carefully. These incidental screws and bolts will come in very handy later.

3. *Play it safe.* Be sure you have an engine hoist and engine stand, as well as a floor jack, even if you have to rent them. Improvising these is time-consuming and dangerous, *so don't do it.* We rented the hoist from a speed shop and "borrowed" the stand and floor jack from a friend for a minimum amount of cash.

Reassembling an engine is definitely a complicated thing to do. An engine has dozens of parts, and they all have to be put in correctly. If they're not, you might snap a part or a whole series of parts when you try to start the engine.

The keys to assembling an engine are care and patience. Remember an engine is not an unsolvable mystery; it's a bunch of parts that have been linked together one after the other. What's more, the people who build and repair engines aren't any smarter than you; they've become skilled through putting engines together over and over again.

First, read the instructions in your books or the ones that come with the parts. Then read them again. Next, visualize the sequence of actions. You should read the instructions and visualize what will happen several times. When the procedures feel familiar, you're ready to begin the assembly for real. If you take your time and follow the directions precisely, you'll see an engine gradually take shape. Finally, double-check your work (most repair manuals will tell you ways to check part assembly).

Here are a few other things to think about. Modifying the engine will increase the horsepower of your car. But this is just the first step. You'll want to use this added power as efficiently as possible, and this will mean changes in the exhaust system, transmission, axle, wheels, tires, and brakes. Modifying all of these things at once will be extremely expensive, so some compromises might be in order. This is what we did.

The old exhaust system on the Fairlane was rusted and about to fall off. If we hooked it up to the rebuilt engine, there was a better than even chance it would be blown apart by the huge power increase. Besides, the old exhaust system did not allow exhaust gases to escape the car quickly enough. Gases would back up in the system and eventually in the engine itself, which would reduce performance. The old system had to go.

We found someone selling a set of performance headers through a newspaper ad and bought the set (at about half the price of new headers). We attached these to the heads, then took the car to a muffler shop that specialized in installing pipes and mufflers on high-performance engines. The headers, muffler, and pipes, plus an installation charge, came to $200.

We would have liked to replace the Fairlane's automatic transmission with a four-speed clutch. Unfortunately, this would have cost at least $750, well beyond our budget. Instead, we had a Ford dealer service the automatic transmission to pass along as much power as possible. The Fairlane's original shifting mechanism was on the steering column. We removed this and installed a floor shifter. This didn't improve performance any, but it looked a little sportier. This cost about $95.

We also would have liked to have put in a different axle, one that would give us a neck-snapping start from the line. But a new axle could cost $650 or more. So we decided to keep the axle and rear gears, while keeping our eyes open for possible bargains. As for the wheels and tires, we felt new ones would accent the fire-charred condition of the exterior so much they would look silly. We put off buying them until the exterior could be repaired and painted.

The one job we did not put off at all was the brakes. The brakes we found in the Fairlane were in surprisingly good condition. Even so, we decided to rebuild them to insure that they could handle the horsepower we would add to the car. Always invest money and time in your car's safety features. After all, there isn't much sense in having a car with extra get-up-and-go unless you can stop it too.

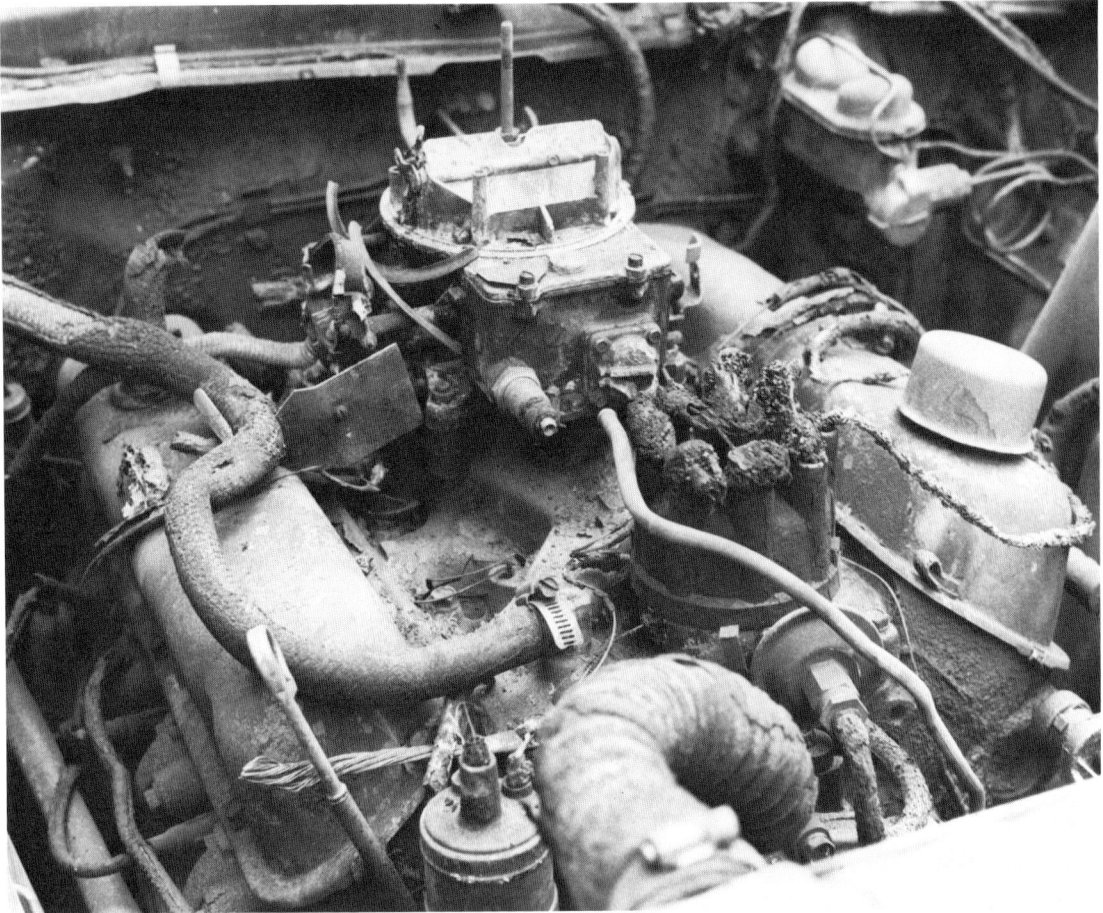

This is dramatic evidence of what an engine fire can do in just a few minutes. Is there a lesson to be learned here? Yes. Every time you tune the engine or change the oil, be sure to check the gas line for leaks. A new piece of gas line might cost you 75¢; a fire might cost you your car.

Loosen and remove the bolts to the transmission and frame, disconnect all of the hoses and wires, and the engine is ready to come out. The engine hoist makes this a relatively easy job. But be careful! The engine is very heavy, and a finger can be crushed easily when maneuvering the engine in the compartment. Here, the engine has been raised, and Tom (on the right) is pulling it away from the car while I keep it from swinging wildly.

We lowered the engine to the ground, resting it in an upright position so we could remove parts from the top first. This position made it easy to remove the flywheel, cylinder covers, manifold, and heads.

Here Tom removes the old manifold. We planned to replace almost all of the parts on and in the engine except the block, flywheel, crankshaft, and oil pan. Even so, Tom is being very careful. The manifold is heavy and could fall and damage the block. And many of these old parts might be useful, if not in the Fairlane, then in some other way. For instance, we traded the old cylinder heads and a little cash for ones already rebuilt for a 289 high-performance engine. We didn't save a great deal of money, but we were spared hours of work.

When as much as possible of the top of the engine had been removed, we turned the engine over and began taking out the oil pan bolts. The oil pan will then be scrubbed clean and reused. To the left of the engine is a small plastic flowerpot where we stored engine bolts. Even if you intend to put in new bolts, it's smart to keep the old ones until the project is over.

The pistons had frozen stuck in the cylinders due to rust. Here Tom gently taps on one to free it. Again, care has to be taken. Why? The old piston heads had been destroyed, but the connecting rods could be used again. And since a set of rods can cost from $75 to $150 each, it makes sense to save the rods.

After every part had been removed, we took the engine block to a machine shop to have it boiled clean. This rids the block of every speck of dirt and oil and washes away even tiny bits of metal that might scratch the cylinder walls, piston heads, cam, and crankshaft bearings.

You might be tempted to begin assembling the engine on the ground, but resist this notion. Your work on the engine will go more smoothly and quickly if the block is attached to an engine stand. After putting the block on the stand, we began the serious work. First we had to clean carbon deposits from the tops of the cylinders. This close-up shows a ridge reamer in action. The ridge reamer has a sharp blade that cuts away the deposits as it is turned in the cylinder.

Next we used a cylinder hone attached to an ordinary drill to scour the cylinder walls until the metal was perfectly smooth and shiny. The cylinder on the left has been cleaned, while the two to the right wait their turn.

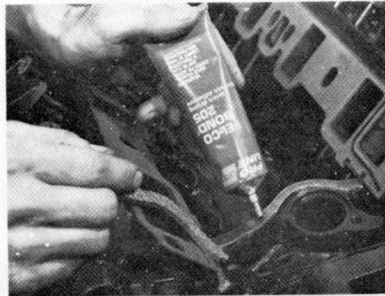

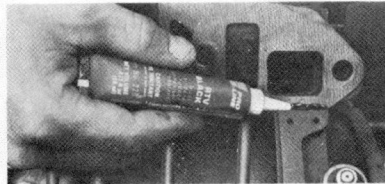

There are a lot of parts in an engine, and each has to be installed *exactly* as the directions specify, so take your time. Most new parts come with illustrated instructions, such as these for putting in various gaskets and seals. Books on repairs and rebuilding also come in handy. They usually provide lots of details and step-by-step illustrations, plus they might tell you how to check that the parts have been installed correctly.

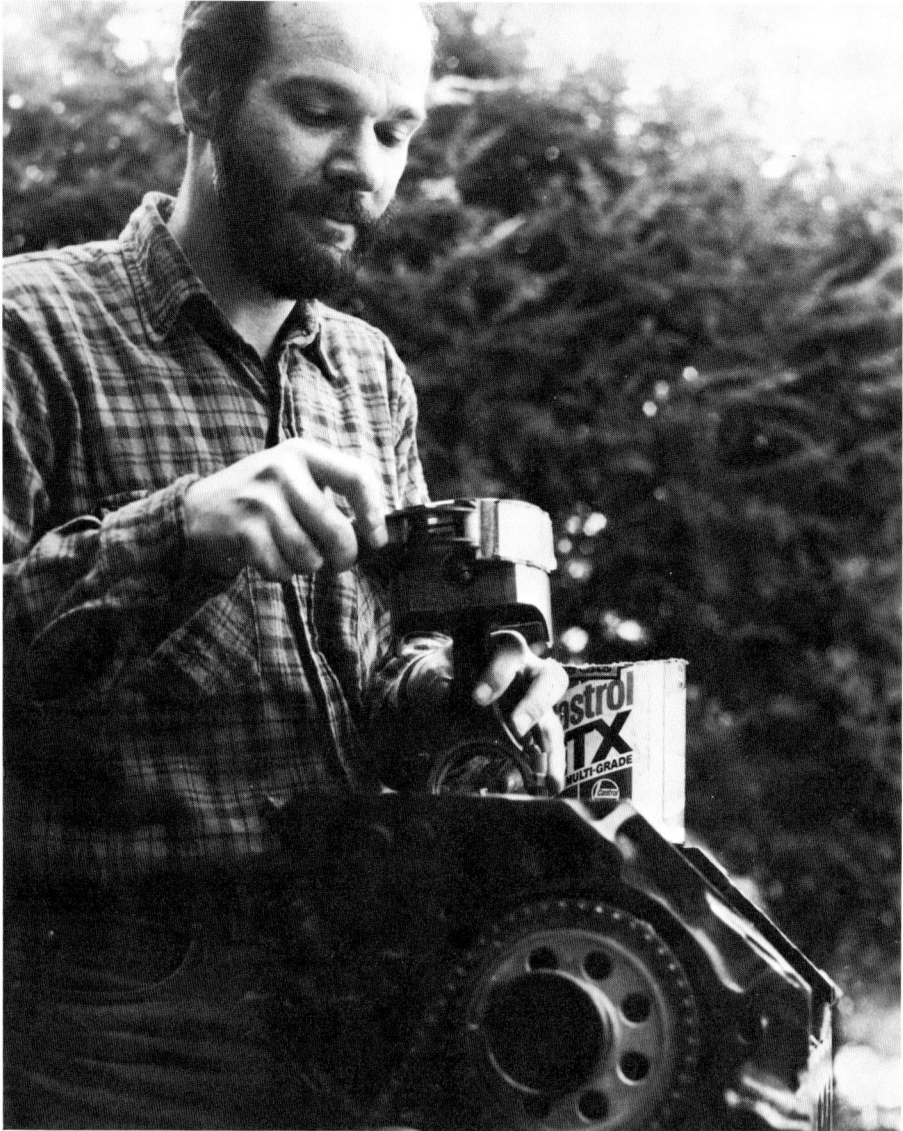

Now the engine is ready for assembly. The crankshaft and camshaft went in first; then the timing chain was connected to these two parts. This photo shows a piston being inserted in the cylinder with the help of a piston ring compressor. It holds the three piston rings flush to the piston wall so the piston can be inserted into the cylinder easily. The rings then expand to keep oil in the crankshaft area from seeping into the combustion chamber.

With the pistons installed, the heads can be bolted on. The torque wrench allows the head bolts to be tightened to a specific pounds-per-square-inch designation. This means the head will be on evenly, that no one bolt will be tighter than another. If one bolt were loose, the massive pressure created by the explosion of gas in the combustion chamber would cause a pressure leak, which would severely affect engine performance and possibly damage the engine.

Here the cylinder valves are being adjusted to a precise measurement. One valve allows gas vapors to enter the combustion chamber; the other lets exhaust fumes escape. The more precisely the openings and closings of these valves are set, the more efficiently the engine will run.

We wheeled the engine stand out into the sun to finish up the work. The manifold was bolted on, then came the distributor cap, water pump, alternator and power steering pump, belts and fan, valve covers, and headers. This photo shows us working on the carburetor.

We hooked the engine to the hoist, which allowed us to take it off the engine stand. Then we bolted on the transmission. Now it's ready to go back into the car.

4

Lookin' Good

We'd popped the engine out and begun gathering and assembling the parts. This is plenty to keep anyone occupied for weeks and weeks. But even as this area of work progressed, we launched into another: getting the engine compartment ready.

Cleaning and refinishing an engine compartment isn't on every customizer's "must do" list. It's a nasty, dirty job, and many people simply don't feel it's worth the time or energy. We did for a number of reasons. The fire had destroyed every wire and part under the hood, including the battery, ignition coil, windshield wiper motor, and radiator hoses. Replacing these and rewiring would be made simpler if the compartment were clean. A clean engine compartment would also highlight the new engine. Finally, we knew the job wouldn't cost much at all; the bill for cleaning fluid, steel wool, sandpaper, and two cans each of spray primer and paint came to only $35.

A few fast words. First, be prepared to get very dirty during the cleaning process. This means wearing shoes and clothes you won't mind throwing away and having plenty of cleaning fluid to remove grease, grime, and old paint from your hands and face. You'll also want to lay a large protective tarp on the ground to catch globs of grease and paint. Second, to reduce cost, you can use canned spray primer and paint. Whenever you paint, be sure you do it in a well-ventilated area. If you follow the directions on the can carefully, you can produce a remarkably smooth finish. But no matter how perfect your canned paint finish looks in the engine compartment, don't for a moment consider doing the exterior that way. You can tolerate small painting imperfections in the engine compartment; the exterior should be perfect.

Once the engine compartment was done and the engine in and running, we turned our attention to the exterior. Put simply, the Fairlane's body was in wretchedly poor condition. Rust had taken a severe toll on much of the metal, especially around the wheels; there were dents, scrapes, gouges, and gings in every part of the car, including the roof. Worse, someone had done a sloppy, amateurish repair job on the two left side doors and back panel.

Pulling out dents, filling in holes, fashioning new wheel wells, and rust-proofing require an enormous degree of skill, and doing these jobs incorrectly can cause even more damage. Applying spray paint, especially the enamel paint we would eventually choose, is a tricky procedure. And to do the job we would have to rent painting nozzles and hoses, plus the compressor to create enough pressure for an even, consistent spray. To rent this equipment costs about $85 per day. Since we'd be teaching ourselves everything, we could foresee a time-consuming trial-and-error operation, and the rental bill would mount quickly. So, reluctantly, we decided to turn the body work and painting over to an expert.

Don't be discouraged, however, from attempting your own exterior work, especially if your car is in relatively good shape. As always, researching how these jobs are done and getting tips from those experienced in the field are essential. If you find you have an aptitude for these jobs, you'll reap the rewards of solid savings. If not, don't be disappointed. The majority of customizers turn over the exterior work to a professional.

While we wanted someone else to do the work, we didn't want to turn over complete control to that person. So we set about designing the "look" of the car. In order to accent the clean lines of the car and to make it appear lighter, we stripped off all the chrome moldings. For the color, we chose the brightest true red we could find. This happens to be the same red used on Porsches, so tracking down the correct color wasn't hard at all. We knew that a totally red car might be a little overwhelming, so we decided to break up the color with a black front grill and bumper and a twenty-inch-wide black hood stripe.

Once we had a clear image of the car we wanted, we went searching for the person to make it a reality. We looked up the addresses of local body shops and took the car in for estimates. A good price is important, but a top-notch job is even more essential. Before you let anyone work on your car, study some examples of their work. Our search for estimates brought in projected prices of from $2,800 to $3,500. Fortunately, along the way we learned about a guy named Tom Ratkowski who worked in his home garage. We found out that he was often hired to repair new cars that have been damaged during shipping to dealers, which means he has to do excellent work. Since he only worked at night, he made it clear it would take him several months to repair the body damage and do the painting. But his price was worth the wait: $1,800.

While the exterior was being worked on, we began hunting for the wheels and tires. This might seem like a simple enough chore, but the potential expense should make anyone take lots of time. Intead of going top of the line on the tires, we went for much less expensive (but still good) tires, Cooper Pro 70s. They cost $45 each. The wheels were another matter. We wanted wheels that would grab attention and yet be compatible with the straightforward look of the car. Cragar SS/T chrome wheels seemed like the perfect choice.

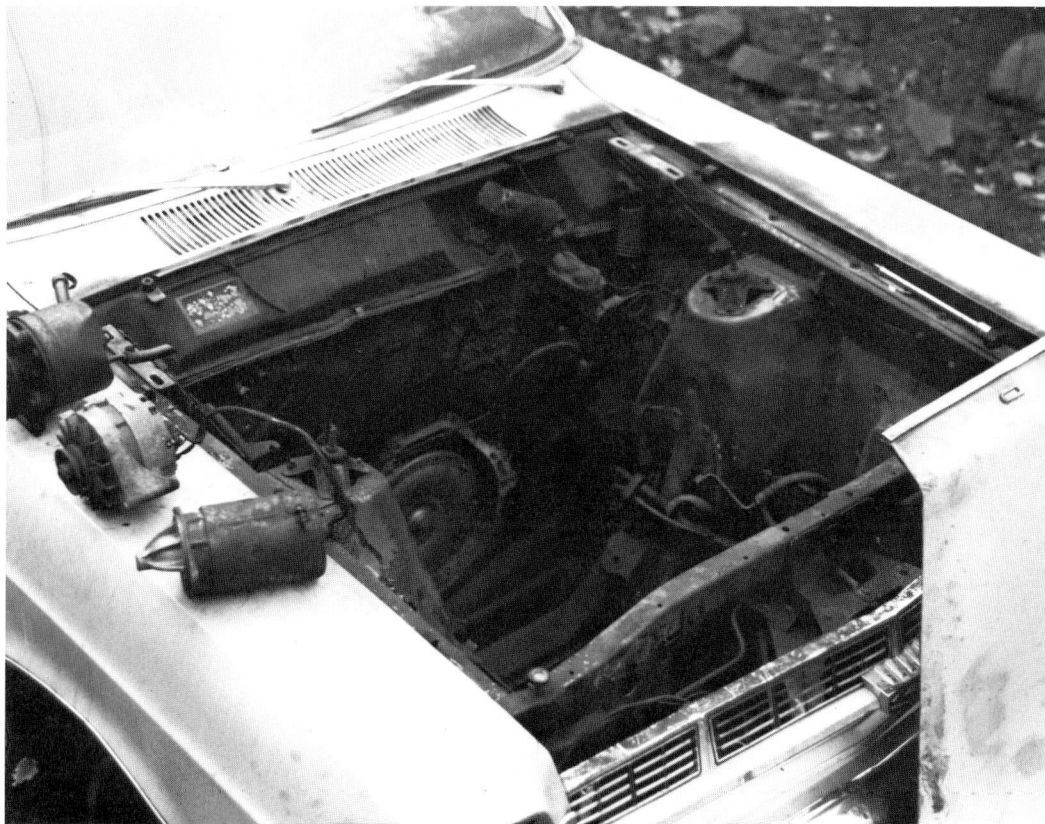

This overhead photo of the engine compartment shows two things. First, it's easy to see how dirty and tired the compartment looks. Second, with the engine out, it's possible to climb in, which makes cleaning, sanding, and painting it a little easier.

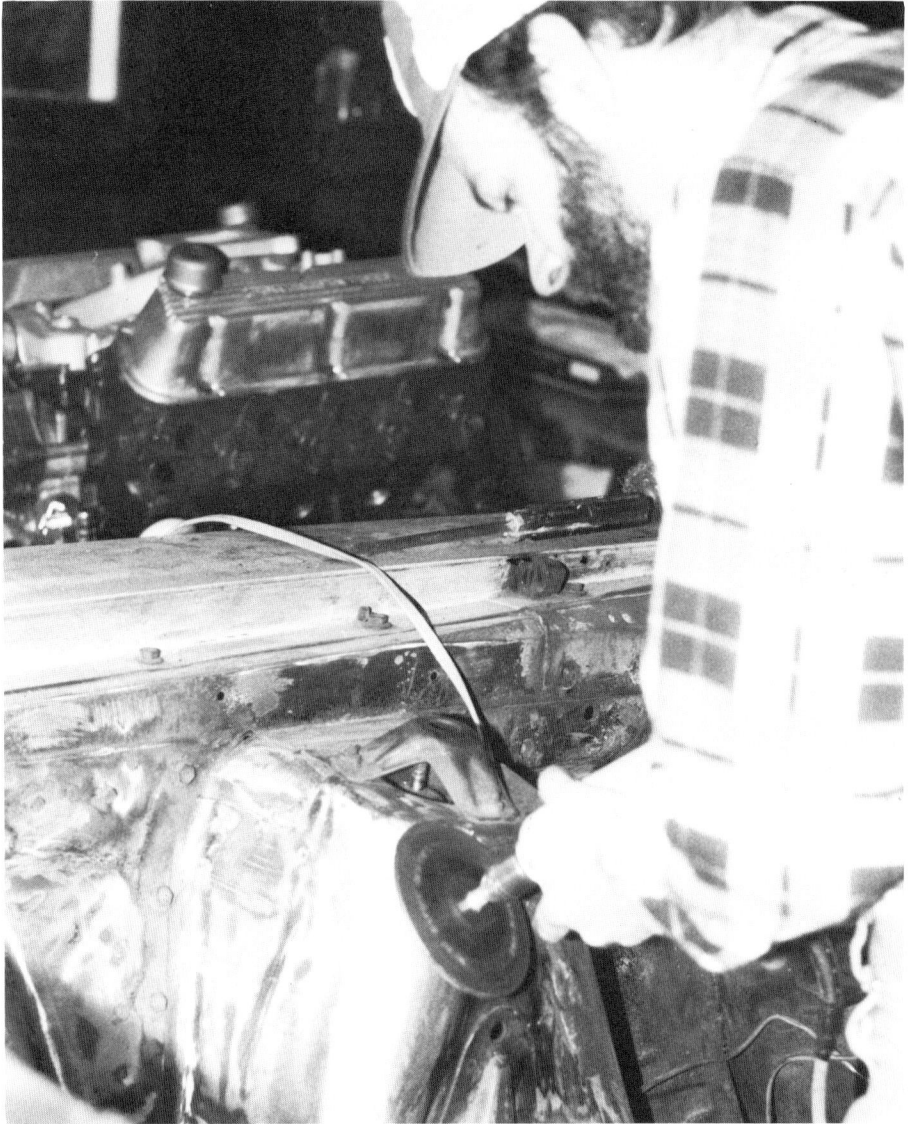

Redoing an engine compartment is very simple. We began by scrubbing the entire inside with a solvent to remove oil and grime. Then we took an ordinary drill and sanded all of the metal until it shone like new.

After this, two coats of canned primer were applied.

This was followed by two coats of satin black paint. The primer goes on very easily because it's thin. But spray paint is a little trickier; it's thick and tends to drip easily. It's best to practice with it on small areas, wiping off drips before they dry. With patience and practice you'll find a spraying rhythm that lays down paint but doesn't cause drips. A hint: you'll want to cover (mask off) the areas you don't want painted with tape and newspaper. This is annoying and time-consuming, but it will make for a cleaner job and sharp lines between the engine compartment and exterior fenders.

Dropping the engine and transmission into the freshly painted engine compartment requires patience. Here we've got it halfway in and are trying to gently coax it in farther.

The engine was lowered and wiggled and lowered some more until it slid into position. Even though we were extremely careful, you'll notice a bend in the compartment frame (at left) where the engine rested on it briefly. Fortunately, the metal could be hammered back into shape and the paint touched up.

The age and condition of the Fairlane exterior are shown clearly in this and the following photo. In the first, rust has eaten away at the metal just behind one of the tires. Almost all of the metal close to the ground showed similar signs of decay.

Even a quick check of this side view reveals the extent of the body damage.

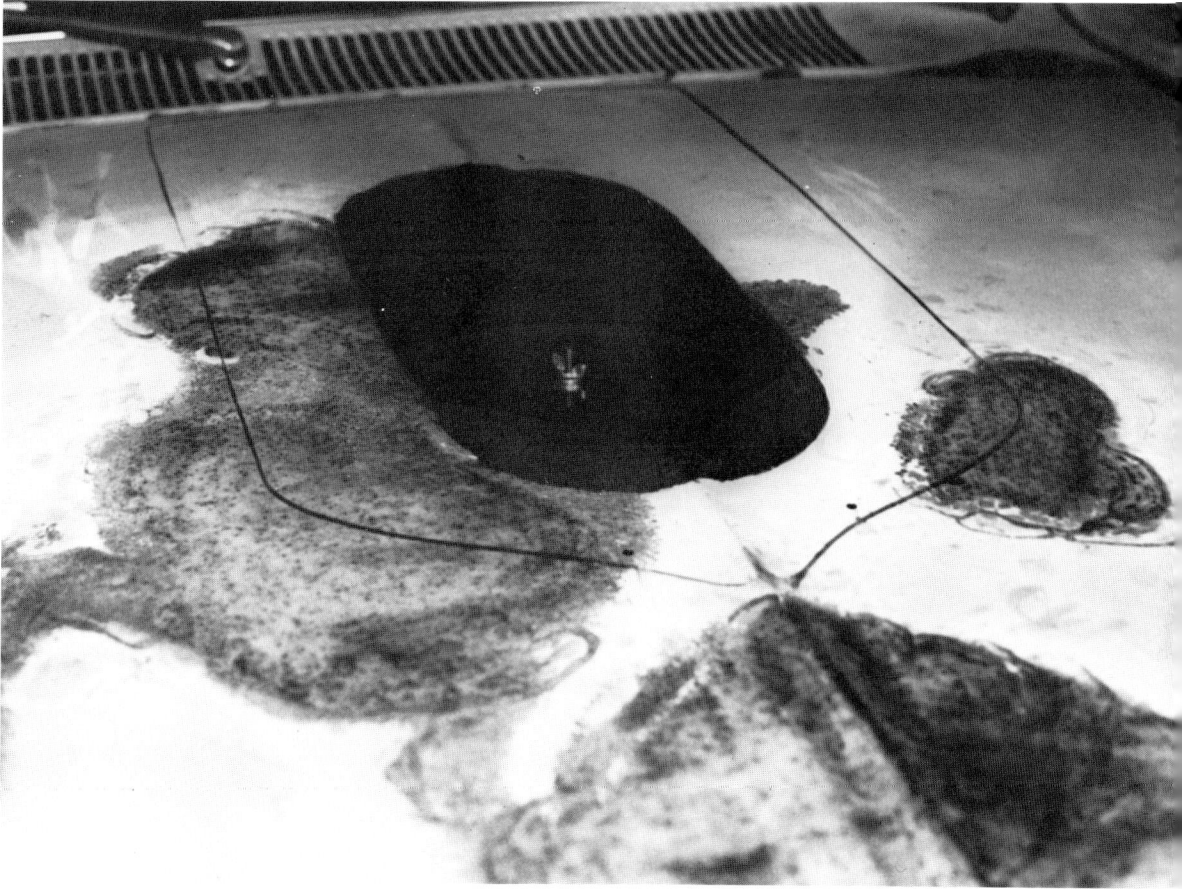

Since we had decided we wouldn't be able to do the body work and painting ourselves, we found someone who could, Tom Ratkowski. He decided to work on the hood scoop first. An outline of the scoop was drawn on the hood and the vent hole cut out.

The bottom part of the scoop has been riveted in place. The fire that destroyed the engine was so hot it warped the hood. As you can see, a great deal of plastic putty had to be used to fill in the depressions; then it was sanded smooth and primed.

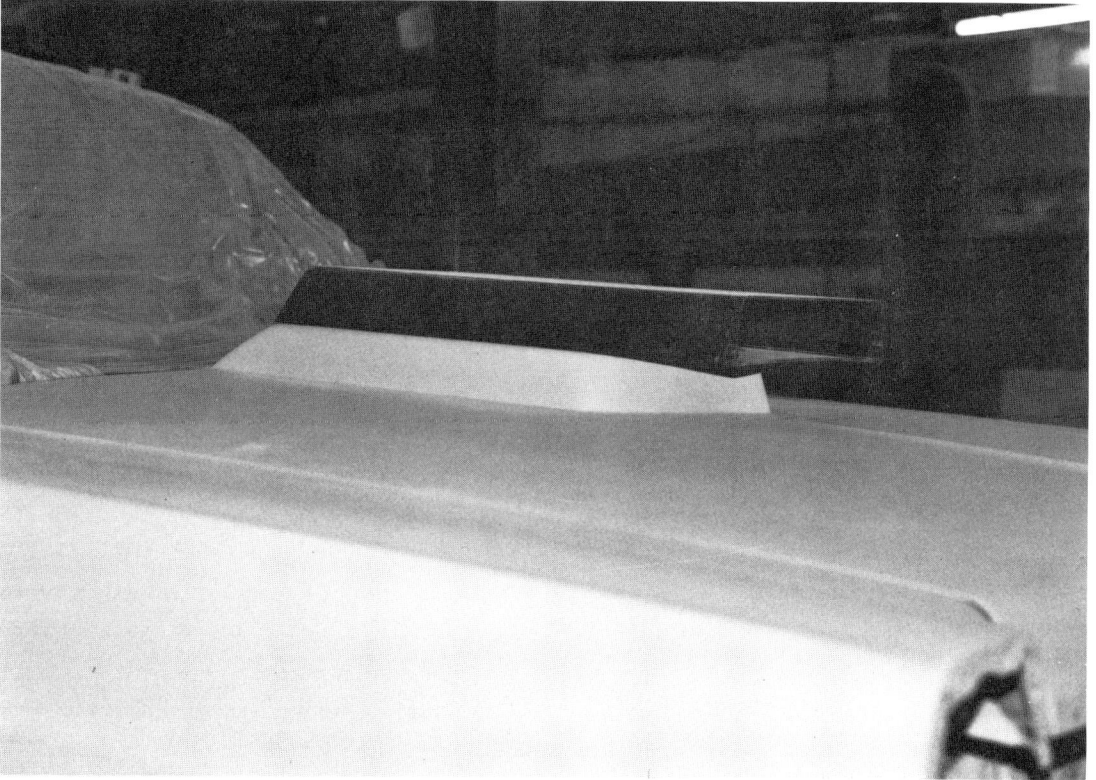

After this, the top of the scoop was riveted on also. It was primed just after this photo.

Here is a close-up picture of the finished hood and hood scoop. By the way, the scoop does more than just take up space. It channels cool air directly into the carburetor, producing a richer air-gas mixture. The result is a more powerful explosion and a gain of about seven horsepower.

Every section of the car went through the same painstaking process as the hood and hood scoop. For instance, here is a photo of a rear quarter panel.

Tom Ratkowski cut away the metal until he found some that had not been eaten away by rust. Then he took a piece of sheet metal that fit the area cut away and welded it in place. After this, he had to hammer the metal to resemble the original contours of the car. Here he melts dabs of metal with an acetylene torch to fill in small holes or join pieces of metal.

These areas are heated to make the metal soft and are gently tapped into shape.

A finished rear panel — the rust is gone, the lines are sharp, and the metal smooth and shiny.

Inch by inch, the body was mended and primed. Finally, the red enamel paint was sprayed on—and a "new" car emerged. The car looked stunning and yet it wasn't complete. It needed sideview mirrors and wheels and tires to give the car a truly finished look.

A plastic guide allowed us to position the mirrors and mark precisely where the screws would go.

Still, we were extremely nervous about drilling into the newly painted car.

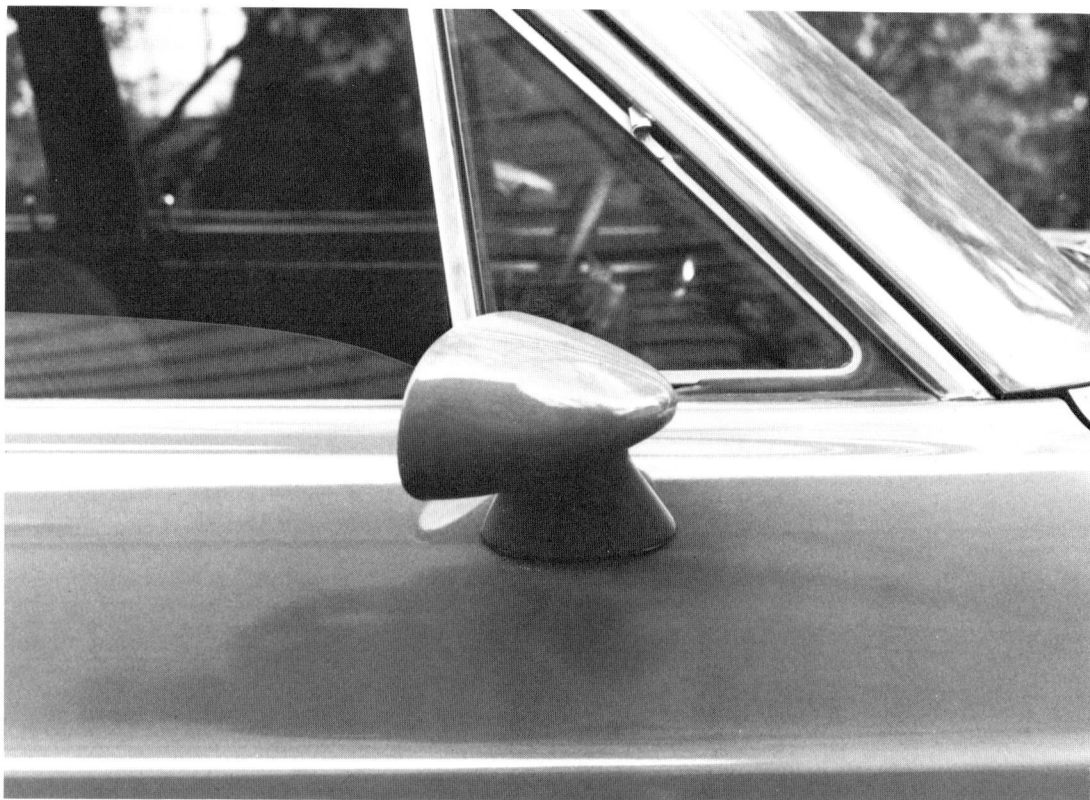

The mirrors provide a wider view of the road behind the car and look sleek besides.

These wheels and tires have seen a lot of miles in their time.

These Cragar SS/T wheels and Cooper tires are a sharp and glittering contrast to the old ones.

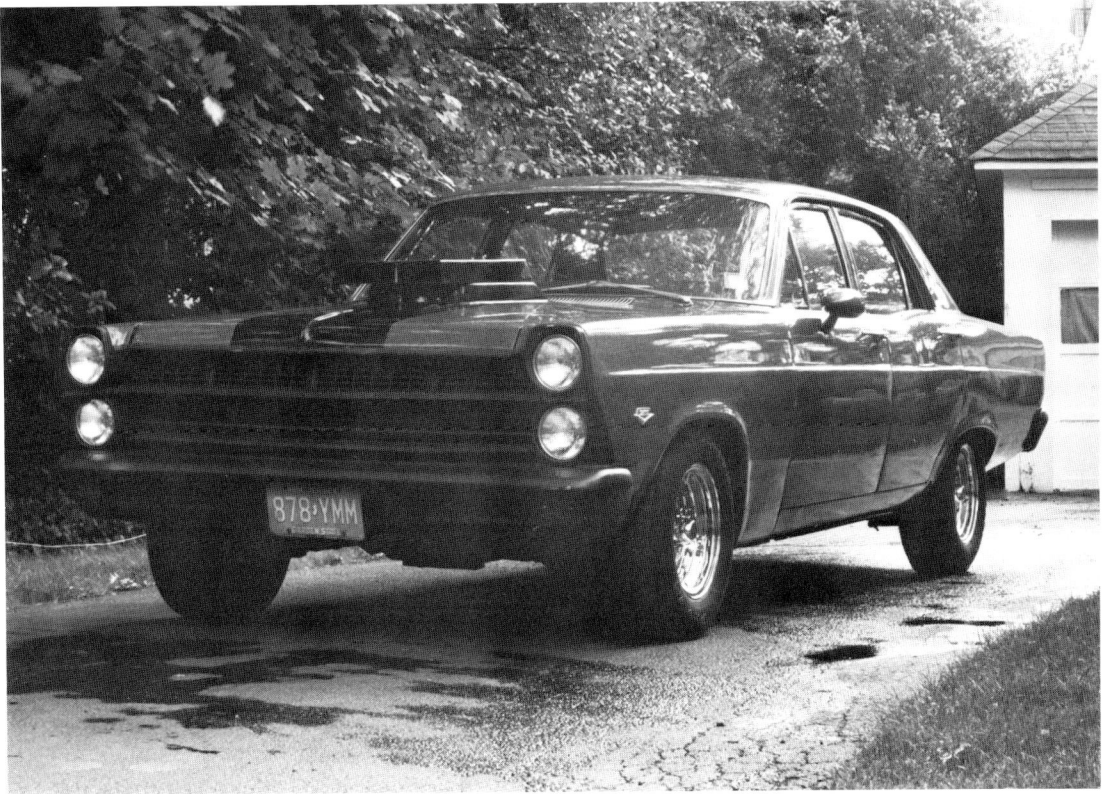

The exterior is finished, and the car is ready to take to the road in style.

5

The Inside Story

The interior should be a customizer's last concern. If you're lucky, the interior that comes with your car will be usable. Its color won't clash hideously with the new exterior, and the carpet and seat covers will be in good condition. Live with it if you can.

The Fairlane, however, was another story. The bland beige interior, complete with singe marks on the dashboard from the fire, was an eyesore. It detracted from the brilliant red exterior and begged to be changed.

But we had a problem. We'd indulged ourselves with the engine rebuilding, the body work, and the painting. In short, we'd eaten up most of the budget. How to make the interior compatible with the rest of the car and do it cheaply was the question.

Simplicity of design was the first step. Aside from a few bits of chrome around the instrument panel and a silver center for the steering wheel, we decided to go with a black interior. This would eliminate mixing and matching colors, something that often requires buying custom-made items. Black is a basic color, and every company produces black parts, such as carpets, seat covers, and headliners. This also means ready availability for these items and competitive prices.

The next step was to retain as much of the interior as possible. We would have liked to have put in bucket seats, but new ones can cost $250 apiece and up. Even going the junkyard route might set us back $75 to $100 per seat. For the time being we would have to be content with recovering the existing bench seats. Even something as seemingly small as the door and window handles can become expensive. A visit to a speed shop revealed that new ones would run at least $30 per door. Polishing up the old ones seemed like a smart and cost-effective (cheap) alternative.

Of course, some things would have to be bought. The seat covers, carpet, and headliner (the fabric that covers the roof of the interior) were all beige and in poor condition. We searched speed shops, stores specializing in covering seats and carpeting cars, and car magazines. We were never satisfied with the materials used by these places or the prices. In the end, we turned to the J. C. Whitney catalog.

As mentioned earlier, the J. C. Whitney catalog carries a wide variety of basic parts. Since we weren't looking for anything exotic or customized, this turned out to be a perfect source for us.

The only other part we planned to purchase was the steering wheel. J. C. Whitney and many advertisers in magazines offer steering wheels and at good prices. But this was one item we wanted to examine firsthand to be sure we liked it. Speed shops usually have a variety of steering wheels in stock; you should visit several shops until you find the perfect steering wheel.

What about the rest of the interior—the dashboard, door paneling, and other metal and vinyl coverings? We could have used special-ordered replacements, but this would have been a real budget buster. We would have to do these ourselves.

Again, canned spray metal and vinyl paint would do, both of which can be found in hardware stores. Since we were going the basic black approach, we had no trouble locating paint. As with all painting jobs, you will want to have lots of ventilation while painting. And read those directions several times.

Estimating the amount of work an interior will require can be hard. The area is very small — you can probably stretch your arms from one side to the other with little effort. But the interior has many different elements, each requiring different tools and techniques.

The best approach is to divide the work into manageable portions. Remove as many parts as possible, such as the door panels, visors, and mirror, and redo them outside the car. Plan on sanding, priming, and painting the dashboard one weekend, a door or two the next. If you pace yourself, you won't be overwhelmed by the amount of work. And after a while, the interior you imagined will begin to become a reality.

Earlier on during our work on the interior, we discovered something very pleasant. Our self-imposed "interior on the cheap" approach was going to cost under $500. We were still under our $5,500 limit for the entire project. So we did what any self-respecting customizer would do. We put in a new stereo-cassette system, complete with four speakers and a hundred-watt amplifier. What's the use of driving around in a rebuilt high-performance car unless you have the tunes to do it with?

Torn, soiled, and sagging, the front seat is an awful sight.

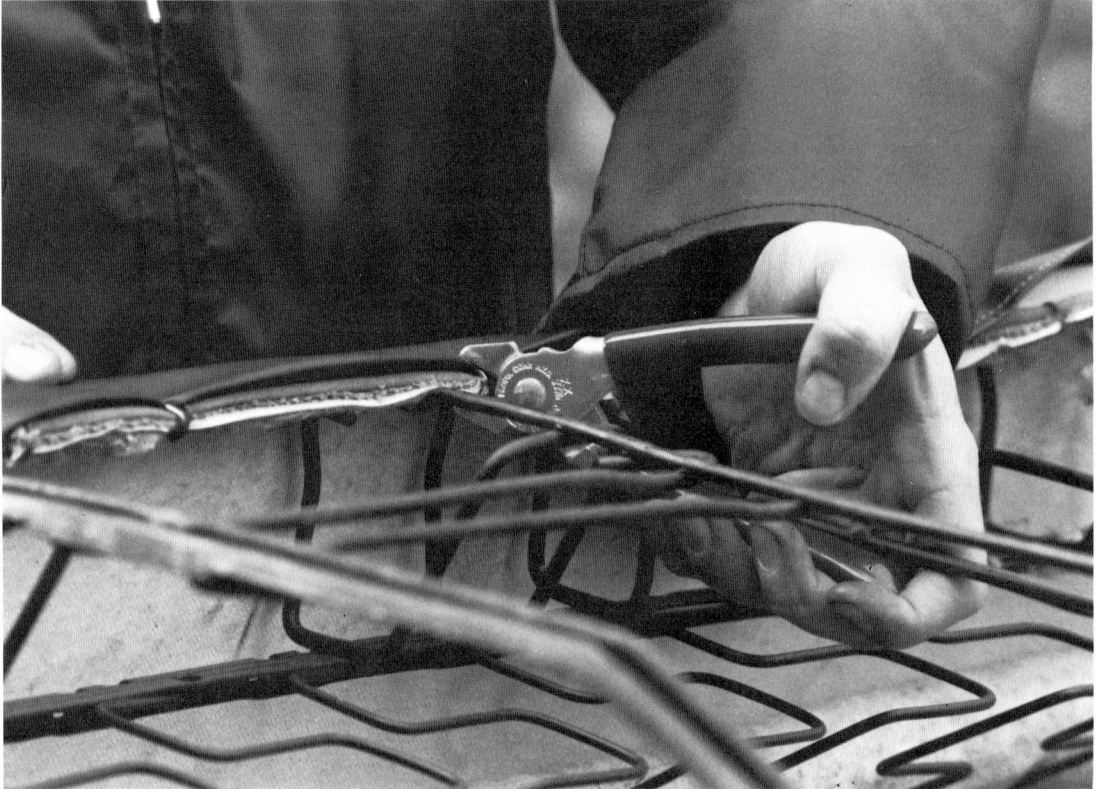

Putting new seat covers on is surprisingly easy. The seats themselves come apart, so each section can be worked on separately. The old covers and padding can be cut off. New padding is cut to fit the contours of the seat; then the new covers are slipped on over the padding. Here is a close-up of the new seat covers being hog riveted in place.

A hog riveter is really just a very strong stapler that secures the seat cover to the wire metal frame. When the seat is reassembled and bolted back in place, the hog rivets will be out of view.

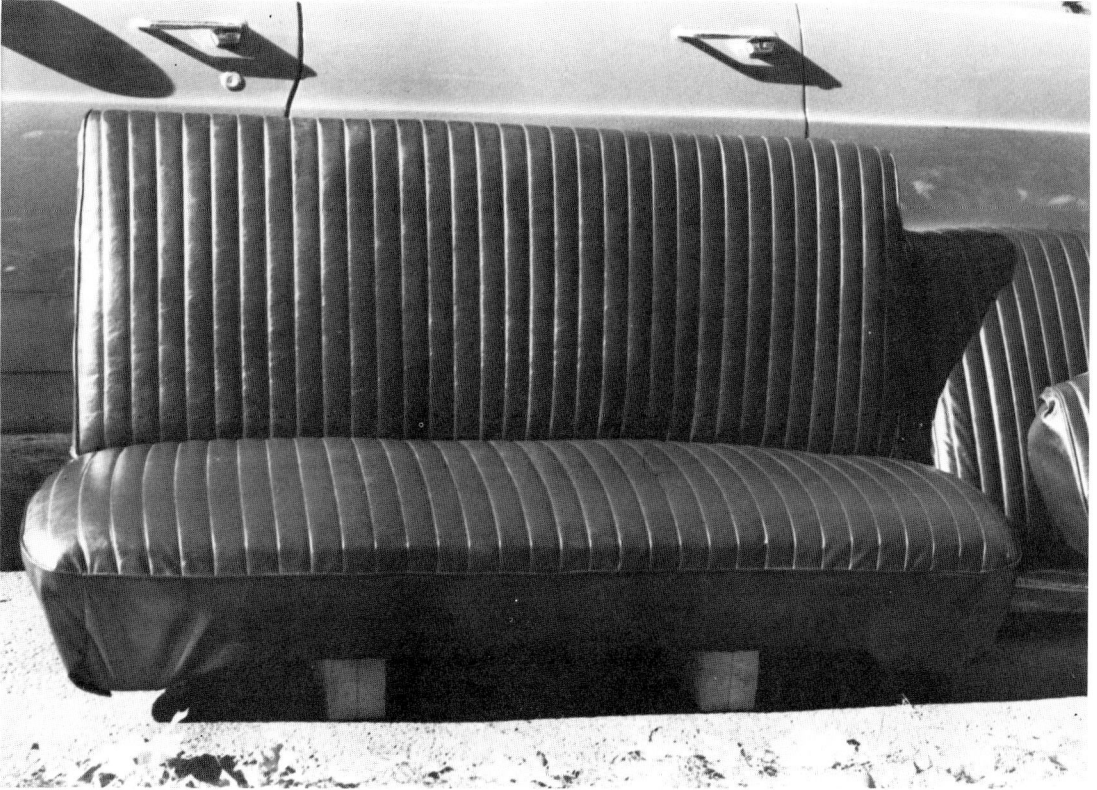

The finished seat is ready to go back into the car.

The doors and door panels weren't as badly beaten up as the seats, but they were the wrong color. We kept the old door handles, but the door cushions were too clumsy looking, so we took them off. Doing this left a slightly irregular pattern in the panel, but we still felt it was better than keeping the cushions. We removed the door panel and painted it outside of the car.

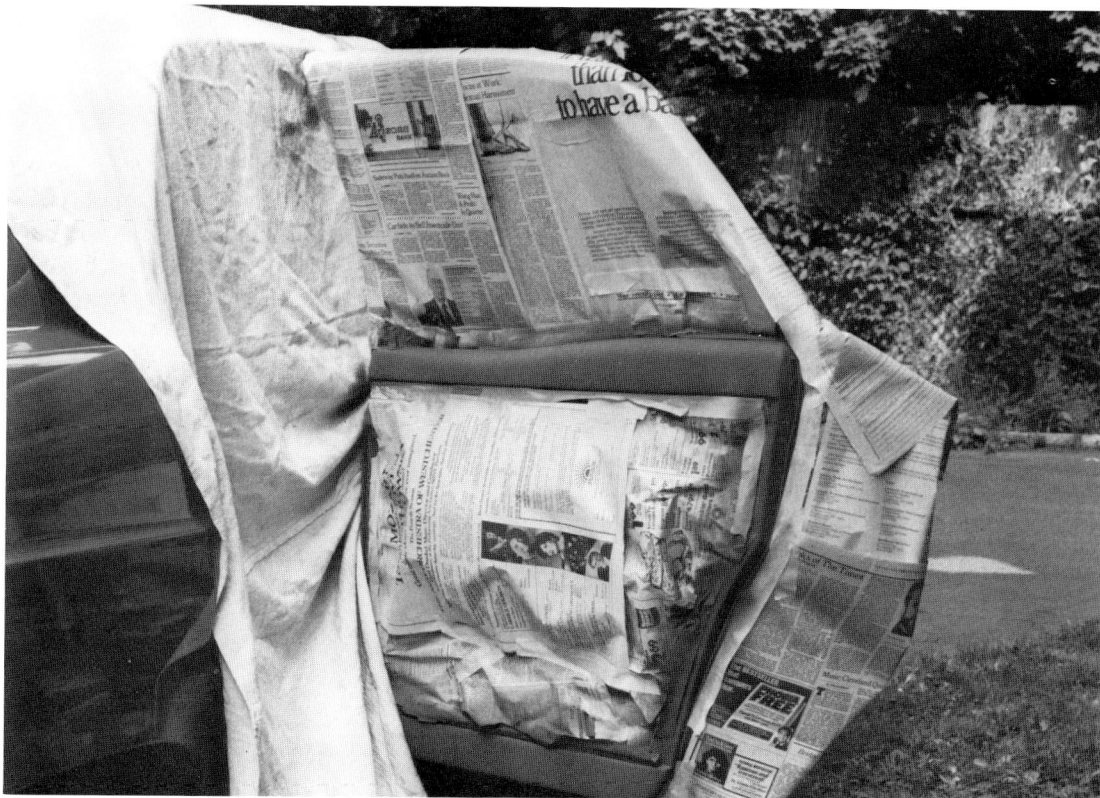

We sandpapered all of the metal on the door, then taped newspaper over everything we didn't want painted. We also protected the exterior with large drop cloths. This is an instance where you can't overdo the protection! At the time of this photo, the primer has been applied and is drying.

The metal has been painted, the panels installed—a new door is the result.

A "before" shot of the dashboard. It's heavy with chrome.

A lot has happened to the dash already. We stripped off as much of the old chrome as possible. We removed the old radio and filled the space with gauges for oil pressure, water temperature, and amps. To the left of these gauges (and slightly hidden by the old steering wheel) is a tachometer to show the number of engine revolutions per minute. This will help us monitor engine performance. While the interior work wasn't finished, we had already ordered all of the parts and knew we'd come in under budget. The stereo-cassette and amplifier were our reward for holding down the costs on the interior.

The old, hard plastic steering wheel has been yanked off, and Tom is attaching the new one. The new steering wheel is black with a silver center, a color combination that seemed to fit the look of the renovated interior.

No one would ever claim that the dashboard is elegant. But it is new and durable and does complement the look and image of the rest of the car.

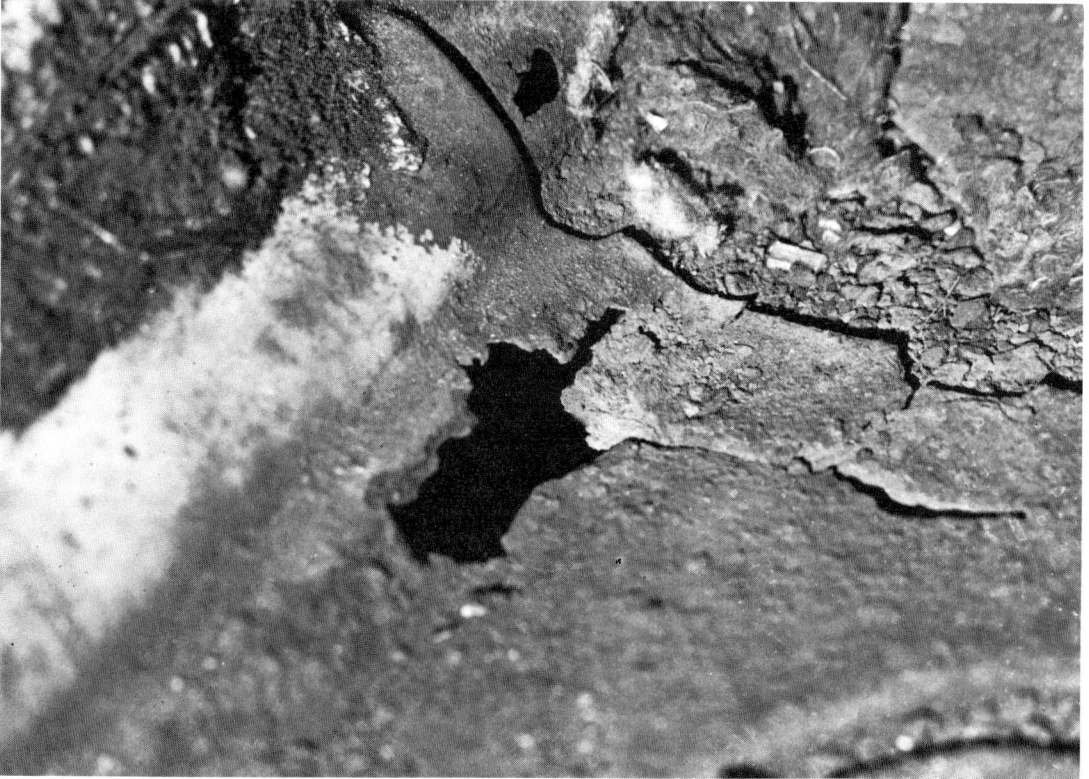

The final step was to put in the carpet. We ran into a little surprise, however. When we pulled up the old carpet, we discovered severe rust in the floor. The answer to this problem was simple and inexpensive.

We bought a piece of sheet metal and cut it to cover the rust. It was hammered to fit the contours of the floor, then riveted into place.

After the floor was repaired, we glued a thick padding on top. This not only softens the floor, but it muffles engine and road noise. Then the carpet was installed. Here the front section of the carpet is being pushed to fit the shape of the interior floor and walls.

6

The Fairlane Is Finished- or Is It?

We'd taken a beige, burned-out bomb of a car and redone it inside and out. Whenever we pulled in to get gas, the attendants asked to see the engine. Truck drivers blew their horns when we went past and gave us the thumbs-up signal of approval. We'd done it. We'd finished the Fairlane. Or had we?

Almost as soon as we'd "finished," we began thinking of stiffening up the rear springs and shock absorbers so the car would handle better. We also began looking around for different rear end gears and a manual clutch transmission. And, of course, the engine needed constant attention and care to keep it running smoothly and efficiently.

We also had some unexpected work to do. Within the space of two months, someone stole the battery and someone else threw a rock through a side window. Not only did we have to replace these parts, but we decided to put in a security system before anything worse happened to the car. Remember, most people will admire your car, but some will view it as a target.

In truth, the work on a custom car is never finished. But it is work that pays off with a real sense of pride and accomplishment. Every time someone asks, "Hey, what's under the hood?" or when heads turn as you rumble past, you'll know you've done something different and unusual. You've created a custom car.

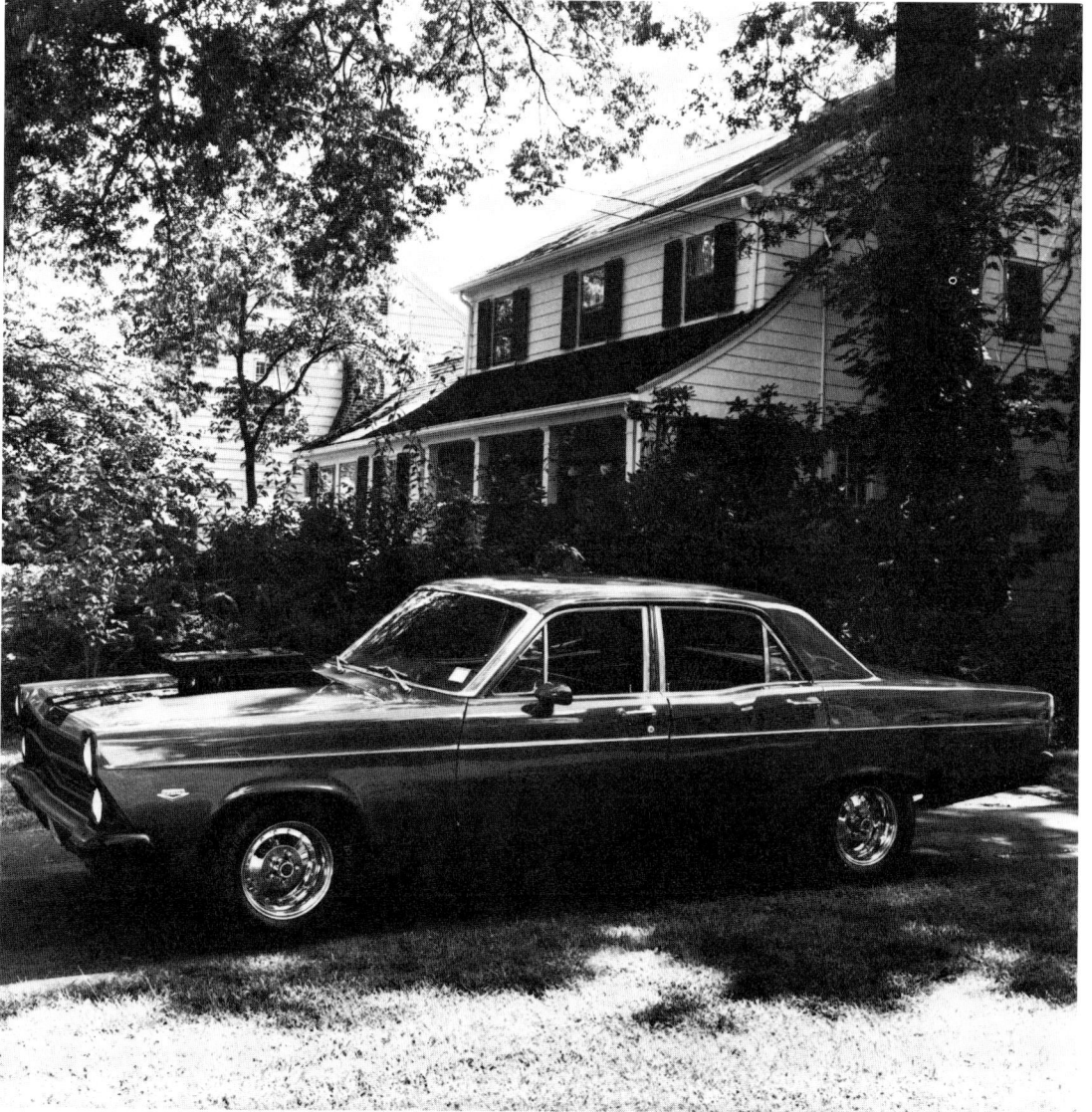

Jon Rosen

Glossary

This book contains a lot of odd or unfamiliar words — camshaft, odometer, manifold, to name a few. To help out, we've prepared the following list of terms that appear in this book. Don't worry about memorizing each definition. As you work on your car, these words will become more and more familiar to you.

Air filter: A metal and paper device designed to keep debris from entering and clogging the engine.

Alternator: A belt-driven motor attached to the engine block that converts mechanical energy into electricity and charges the battery.

Axle: A metal shaft on which the wheels are bolted. The *drive axle* is the shaft that passes power along to wheels and is usually in the rear of older model cars.

Battery: A device for generating and storing an electrical current by chemical reaction.

Bumpers: Either of two horizontal metal structures attached to the front and rear of a car to absorb the impact of a collision.

Camshaft: A metal shaft with lobe-shaped knobs to open and close engine valves.

Carburetor: The part of the engine where air and gasoline are mixed and passed along to the manifold.

Clutch: See *power train.*

Combustion chamber: See *cylinders.*

Connecting rods: A metal rod or arm that connects the piston to the crankshaft.

Crankshaft: A large, rotating shaft in the engine that converts the up-and-down motion of the pistons to rotary motion and passes it along to the power train.

Cylinders (also combustion chamber): The place in the engine where the air-gas mixture is exploded to move pistons up and down.

Distributor: Circular device on engine that sends electric current to cylinders to ignite the air-gas mixture.

Exhaust system: The group of parts (headers, exhaust pipes, mufflers, and tail pipes) that carry gas fumes from the engine to the rear of the car.

Fender: The portion of automotive body work near each wheel. Generally, the front sections are referred to as fenders, while the rear sections are called quarter panels.

Floor shifter: A stick device attached to the transmission and used to put the car in forward, reverse, or neutral.

Flywheel: A large, rotating wheel attached to the crankshaft that minimizes the speed variations of the crankshaft.

Gas line: The hose that conveys gasoline from the gas tank to the carburetor.

Gaskets: Flat rubber or cork sheets used as a seal between two metal surfaces to prevent gas or liquid from escaping.

Headers: A series of specially designed exhaust pipes that are bolted directly onto the engine. Headers help get exhaust fumes out of and away from the cylinders to facilitate a cleaner ignition of the air-gas mixture.

Headliner: A vinyl covering attached and glued to the roof of the interior.

Hood scoop: A specially designed opening in the hood that

allows a larger quantity of air to flow to the air filter and carburetor.

Ignition coil: A device that takes low voltage from the battery and alternator and builds it up to a high enough voltage to ignite the air-gas mixture.

Manifold: The part that takes the air-gas mixture from the carburetor and distributes it to the cylinders.

Muffler: The part of the exhaust system that deadens the sound of gas explosions.

Odometer: Instrument on the dashboard used to indicate the number of miles the car has traveled.

Oil pan: Large receptacle attached to the bottom of the engine where oil is stored. The *splash pan* is a metal shield in the oil pan that keeps reservoir of oil from interfering with movement of pistons and crankshaft.

Piston: A solid metal disk in the cylinder that goes up and down as a result of combustion of the air-gas mixture.

Power train: The various parts that transfer engine power to the wheels, including the clutch, transmission, drive shaft, universal joints, and drive axle.

Suspension: The springs, shock absorbers, ball joints, and other devices by which the car is supported on its axles.

Tachometer: A gauge that tells how many times per minute the crankshaft is turning.

Transmission: The system of gears whereby engine power is transferred to the drive axle.

Water pump: Small apparatus on the engine that facilitates the regular flow of water from radiator to engine block.

Wiring harness: Main set of wires that connects the ignition to the rest of the electric system.

Price List

The following is a list of parts and accessories used for rebuilding the Fairlane. The list is fairly comprehensive, though many of the smaller engine parts have been included under the miscellaneous heading for space considerations. Items with an asterisk next to them were new or almost new and found through newspaper ads or friends. The prices are what we paid for the part and will vary according to region and availability.

Car	$75.	Timing chain cover	$35.
		Splash pan (for oil pan)	$32.
Engine and transmission		Water pump	$35.
Cleaning engine		Spark plugs	$12.
block	$43.	Spark plug cables	$25.
Air filter	$26.	Distributor, dual	
Carburetor*	$75.	point	$85.
Manifold*	$100.	Points	$10.
Heads (rebuilt)*	$75.	Fan*	$15.
Pistons and rings	$119.	Fan belts	$20.
Getting pistons pressed		Alternator	$22.
onto rods	$45.	Power steering pump*	$20.
Camshaft*	$15.	Hoses and clamps	$43.
Cam kit*	$70.	Wiring harness*	$10.
Crankshaft parts	$75.	Other incidental	
Timing chain kit	$20.	wiring	$10.

Ignition coil	$29.	Exhaust system	
Starter motor	$39.	Headers*	$50.
Windshield wiper motor*	$20.	Mufflers, pipes, and installation	$150.
Breather caps	$13.		
Valve covers*	$40.	Repair and painting of exterior and interior	
Oil pump	$32.		
Dipstick and assembly*	$5.	Repair, priming, and painting of exterior	
Front cover for engine	$17.	by professional	$1,800.
Battery	$50.	Hood scoop	$80.
Gaskets	$35.	Fender ornaments	$15.
Fuel pump	$30.	Sandpaper, primer, and paint for engine compartment and interior	$35.
Transmission servicing and fluid	$50.		
Shifter*	$45.		
Engine hoist rental ($35 per rental)	$70.	Headliner and glue	$65.
		Carpet	$125.
Engine stand rental	$10.	Sheet metal for floor repair	$10.
Floor jack rental	$25.		
Miscellaneous parts and tools	$100.	Pop riveter for fastening sheet metal to floor	$18.

Brakes, wheels, and tires

Master brake cylinder*	$35.	Seat covers, padding, and hog riveter	$105.
Brake shoes and kit	$43.		
Shock absorbers (front and rear)	$65.	Steering wheel	$50.
		Dashboard gauges	$80.
Wheels (four Cragar SS/T)	$380.	Radio, amplifier, and four speakers	$460.
Tires (four Cooper Pro 70)	$180.		$5,468.

Index

Page numbers in *italics* refer to photograph captions.